The moon (and the stars) for Sarah-Jane and Pauline
and also Jennifer, for her kind help and support

Text and illustrations © 1993 by Rodney Rigby.
All rights reserved. Printed in Hong Kong.
First published in 1992 by ABC, All Books for Children,
33 Museum Street, London WC1A 1LD, United Kingdom.
First published in the United States of America by Hyperion Books for Children,
114 Fifth Avenue, New York, New York 10011.
FIRST EDITION
1 3 5 7 9 10 8 6 4 2
Library of Congress Cataloging-in-Publication Data
Rigby, Rodney.
The night the moon fell asleep/Rodney Rigby — 1st ed.
p. cm.
Summary: A cowboy, an astronaut, a composer, and others in the
town convince the Moon to return to her important place in the sky.
ISBN 1-56282-334-5 (trade) — ISBN 1-56282-335-3 (lib. bdg.)
[1. Moon — Fiction.] I. Title
PZ7.R44178Ni 1993
[E] — dc20   92-15928
CIP
AC

The Night the Moon Fell Asleep

RODNEY RIGBY

Hyperion Books for Children
New York

One night the moon fell asleep . . .

. . . and came crashing to the ground.

"What was that?" everyone asked as they came running.
"The moon has fallen asleep!" someone cried.
"Shhh!" said another. "Don't wake her up."
"But we must," said a third. "Imagine a sky without
the moon." And after imagining for a brief moment,
everyone frantically tried to awaken the moon.
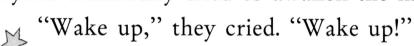 "Wake up," they cried. "Wake up!"

But the moon was in such a deep sleep, she didn't wake up at all.

The doctor was summoned.

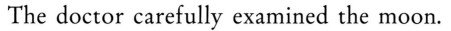

The doctor carefully examined the moon.
"What's wrong with the moon?" everyone asked.
"Well," said the doctor in a very deep and serious
voice, "the moon is tired from too many late nights!"
Everyone sighed a sigh of relief.
"All the moon needs is a good night's sleep,"
prescribed the doctor.

And so, everyone tiptoed home to let the moon sleep.
The next day, everyone returned.

"Good morning, Moon," they said. "Why are you blue?"

"It's so cold and dark and lonely in the sky," she answered. "I won't go back up there!"

"But you must," they all replied. "You must!"

"You expect to see me up in the sky night after night, but no one really cares about me," the moon sobbed.

"O Moon!" said a cowboy, stepping forward. "That's not so. I'd miss you every night if you weren't there. You always keep me company when I'm on the range."

"One person who cares isn't much at all," said the moon sadly.

"O Moon!" said an astronaut, stepping forward. "That's not so. I would miss you every time I blast off into space if you weren't there. I love traveling to see you."

The moon smiled
a little, but she still
felt blue. "No one else
cares," she whispered.

"O my dear Moon!" said a great composer, leaping forward. "That's not so. I would miss you every time I sat at my piano. You always inspire me to write such lovely music."

"We'd miss you watching over us while we sleep," sang out the voices of all the children.

"And we'd miss howling to your full, gleaming face," barked the scruffiest dog.

"O Moon! It's just not the same without you!" insisted everyone.

The moon blushed.

"Well," she said sheepishly, "it's getting dark and there's work to do."

Everyone cheered.

But then the moon looked sad again and she said,

"The sky is such a big place, I'm not sure where I belong. I think I'm lost!"

"O Moon!" said an astronomer, stepping forward.

"I can tell you exactly where you belong."

He looked at his map and
pointed to an empty spot in the sky.
"There," he remarked cheerfully, "that's
where you belong—where we can all see you!"

The moon smiled as she
was gently lifted into the sky underneath
the stars, until she was just high enough.
"Left, a little," shouted the astronomer.
"Left, a little," echoed the crowd.
"Right, a little," instructed the astronomer.
"Right, a little," echoed the crowd.

"Perfect!" cried the astronomer.
"Absolutely!" beamed the moon.
And everyone cheered as loud as they
possibly could. "Hooray for the moon!"
It was very late when they went
home to bed.

Beep!

Very soon, everything was silent. And everyone looked
up into the sky at the moon and sleepily said, "Good night."

"Good night," the moon
replied with a smile. "Sleep tight."